This igloo book belongs to:

....

igloobooks

Published in 2019
by Igloo Books Ltd
Cottage Farm
Sywell
NN6 0BJ
www.igloobooks.com

Copyright © 2018 Igloo Books Ltd
Igloo Books is an imprint of Bonnier Books UK

1019 002
4 6 8 10 11 9 7 5 3
ISBN 978-1-78810-910-9

Written by Melanie Joyce
Illustrated by Richard Watson

Designed by Jason Shortland
Edited by Hannah Campling

Printed and manufactured in China

The Superstar Cow

Written by
Melanie Joyce

Illustrated by
Richard Watson

igloobooks

One morning, on Hedge Bottom Farm, Farmer Bob was eating his toast,
when a fancy-looking letter dropped on the mat, in the post.

Dear Farmer Bob,
Congratulations!

Your cow, Dolly, has been
talent-spotted to star
in our new advert!

Yours sincerely,

The Friendly Cow Company

Morning Moosli

Farmer Bob
Hedge Bottom Farm
Buttercup Lane
Daisyfield

It was from the Friendly Cow Company, who wanted Dolly, his cow, to star in their milk advert. **"Amazing!"** cried Farmer Bob. **"Wow!"**

Just at that moment, outside, Dolly came passing by.
"They're coming to take Dolly away!" was all she heard Farmer Bob cry.

With only half the story, Dolly thought, **"He's going to get rid of me!**
I'll run away and warn everyone not to tell Farmer Bob where I'll be."

Dolly dashed off to the stable, where Horace the horse was chomping.

She was about to explain everything when she heard a **clomp-clomp-clomping.**

"It's Farmer Bob," she gasped.

"Quick, I've got to hide!"

She grabbed Horace's nosebag...

... and hurriedly shoved him inside.

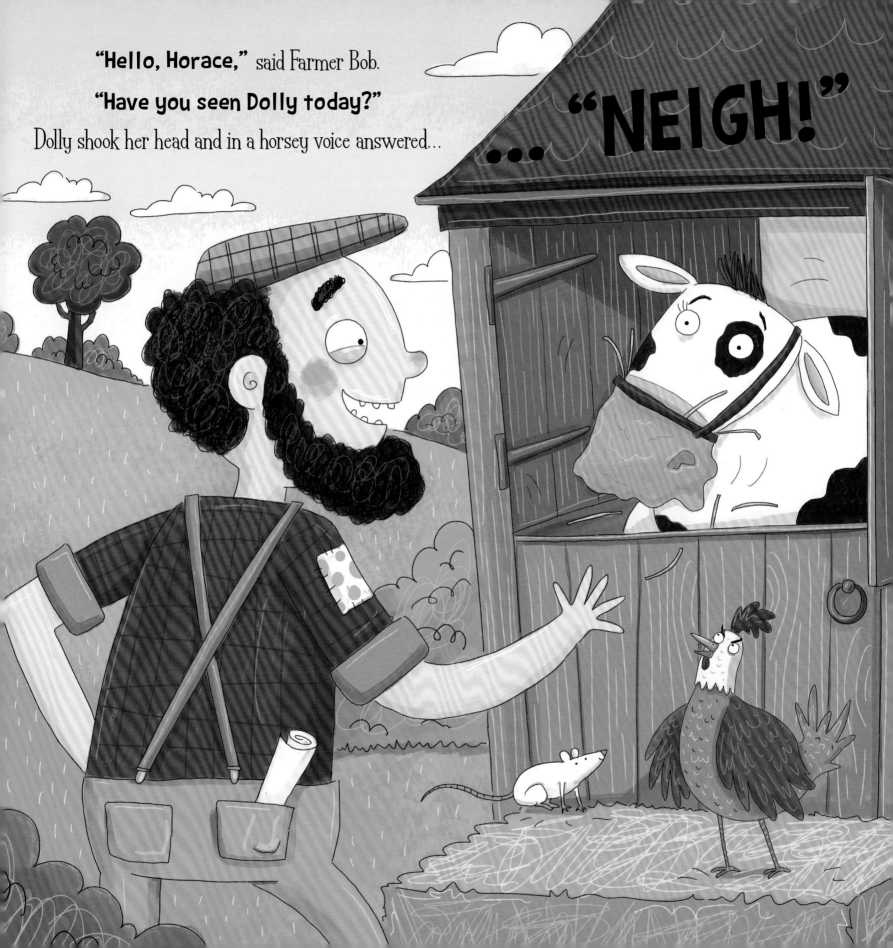

"Hello, Horace," said Farmer Bob.

"Have you seen Dolly today?"

Dolly shook her head and in a horsey voice answered...

... "NEIGH!"

"You don't look well, Horace," said Bob. "Perhaps you should go back to bed."

Farmer Bob **clomped** off to see the sheep.

"I must get there first," Dolly said.

Galloping off to the field, Dolly
frightened the hen and the cat.

She **splashed** through
the sty, leapt over the fence...

... and landed with a **Splat.**

Clomp-clomp-clomp came Farmer Bob. **"I'm looking for Dolly,"** he said.
"What a funny-looking sheep," he thought, staring and scratching his head.

"BAA! Not here!" said Dolly, fibbing. Farmer Bob just stared in alarm.
There was definitely something strange going on at Hedge Bottom Farm.

"The hens will tell me where Dolly is," he said. "They like to gossip all day."

"Uh-oh," said Dolly. "I've got to hurry. Those hens will give me away."

Dolly was feeling so nervous, her tummy **gurgled** and **churned.**
With a blast, she shot off like a rocket, once Farmer Bob's back was turned.

Down the field she **thundered,**

"I can't stop!" she mooed, with a **shout.**

At the henhouse the cockerel

flapped and **squawked,**

"Everybody out!"

There was an enormous **CRASH...** as mud and feathers flew.

Farmer Bob arrived and **gasped,** "Dolly, is that you?"

"YES, it's me!" wailed Dolly. "The one you want taken away."

"Oh, Dolly," said Farmer Bob, hugging her. "You've got it all wrong today."

Farmer Bob told the whole story, so Dolly knew everything was alright.
"They won't want me now," she mooed. **"I look such an awful sight."**

Farmer Bob got some water, some brushes and soft cloths, too.

And everyone helped to make Dolly look just as good as new.

So Dolly went for a makeover and was soon a worldwide star.
Her new advert was shown on screens and billboards near and far.

"Amazing!" cried Dolly's friends.
"You really are famous now."
Dolly of Hedge Bottom Farm had
become a **Superstar Cow!**

THE FRIENDLY COW
COMPANY

THE FRIENDLY COW
COMPANY